Aberdeenshire Library and Information Service
www.aberdeenshire.gov.uk/libraries
Renewals Hotline 01224 661511

KT-429-274

For the real Ellie – and for Ellie's mum – AD
For Nicholas with lots of love – KM

THAT'S NOT RIGHT!
A Red Fox Book: 0 09 943198 X

First published in Great Britain in 2002 by Red Fox
an imprint of Random House Children's Books

3 5 7 9 10 8 6 4

Text copyright © Alan Durant 2002
Illustrations copyright © Katharine McEwen 2002

The right of Alan Durant to be identified as the author and
illustrator of this work has been asserted in accordance with the
Copyright, Designs and Patents Act, 1988.

Red Fox Books are published by Random House Children's Books,
61–63 Uxbridge Road, London W5 5SA,
a division of The Random House Group Ltd,
in Australia by Random House Australia (Pty) Ltd,
20 Alfred Street, Milsons Point, Sydney, NSW 2061, Australia,
in New Zealand by Random House New Zealand Ltd,
18 Poland Road, Glenfield, Auckland 10, New Zealand,
and in South Africa by Random House (Pty) Ltd,
Endulini, 5A Jubilee Road, Parktown 2193, South Africa

THE RANDOM HOUSE GROUP Limited Reg. No. 954009

www.kidsatrandomhouse.co.uk

A CIP catalogue record for this book is available from the British Library.

Printed and bound in Singapore by Tien Wah Press

That's Not Right!

Alan Durant

Katharine McEwen

RED FOX

Ellie's class was writing stories
about animals.

Ellie chose a bug.
This is what Ellie wrote:

Ellie's Story

Once there was a bug. His name was Fred. He lived under a stone.

One day Fred came out. A big shoe stamped down and squashed him.

Splat! Fred was flat.

Fred was dead.
The end.

Ellie read the story to her teacher.

"What a sad story!" the teacher said.
"It has a beginning, a middle and an end," said Ellie.
"So it does," her teacher agreed.

Ellie read the story to her brother.
"That's a funny story," he laughed.

Ellie read the story to her mum.

"What a strange story, Ellie," said her mum.

"It has a beginning, a middle and an end," said Ellie proudly.

Her mum smiled. "Very good, Ellie," she said.

That evening, the moon was full and bright. It was like a giant eye. Ellie sat on the front step to look at it. The moon winked at her.

Something moved on the path in front of Ellie. "Excuse me," said a tiny voice, "but that's not right!"

Ellie looked down and saw a woodlouse.

"I heard your story," said the woodlouse, "and I didn't like it."

"Oh," said Ellie. "What was wrong?"

"It wasn't very nice," said the woodlouse. "Some of my best friends are bugs."

"Oh, I'm sorry," said Ellie. "I didn't mean to upset you."

"What sort of bug was it anyway?" asked the woodlouse.

"One like you," said Ellie.

"I am not a bug," hissed the woodlouse. His antennae waggled crossly. "A bug is a kind of insect. Insects have six legs. I have seven pairs of legs. I am a crustacean, if you must know, like a lobster or a crab."

"Oh," said Ellie. "You don't look like a crab."

"Perhaps not," agreed the woodlouse, "but I do have a hard shell-like body. Lift me up and see."

Ellie put her hand on the ground and the woodlouse crawled onto it. She gazed at the woodlouse. Its body looked a bit like grey armour.

"I see what you mean," she said.

The woodlouse tapped his antennae against her hand. "Now, listen," he said. "I'll tell *you* the story."

16

Fred's Story

There was once a handsome woodlouse called Fred.

He had the finest antennae you ever did see. He lived under a large, cool stone in the garden. His home was dark and damp and lovely. One day Fred was hungry. He crawled out of his house to look for food.

Suddenly, a big, bully shoe stamped
down and tried to squash him. But
Fred was too clever and too quick.
He curled up in a ball and rolled away.
Then he crawled back under his
cool stone and lived happily
ever after.
The end.

"I like that story," said Ellie.

"There's nothing like a happy ending," purred Fred.

Something else moved in the bush beside Ellie.

"That's not right!" a little voice hissed. It was another woodlouse.

"Hello," said Ellie. "Who are you?"

"I'm Mrs Fred," said the woodlouse. "I'm Fred's mate." She waggled her antennae.

"That story just won't do at all," she snorted. "A good story needs more than one character. How could my dear darling Freddy live happily ever after without someone to love?"

"Someone like you?" said Ellie.

"That's right," said Mrs Fred. "Now, dearie, you listen to me."

Mrs Fred's Story

Once upon a time and not so very far away, there lived a lovely woodlouse named Fred. Oh, he was handsome. His antennae were as fine as fine could be. But Fred was not happy. He was all alone in the world. "If only I had someone to love," he said sadly to himself.

Well, one day Fred came out from under his stone to look for food, and what did he spy? Why, a beautiful lady woodlouse!

It was love at first sight. Fred crawled towards her. But then, oh, something terrible happened!

A monster shoe appeared. It stamped down and tried to squash poor Fred.

"Look out!" cried the beautiful lady woodlouse.

Now, luckily, Fred was clever and Fred was quick. In a flash, he curled up in a ball and rolled away.

Wham!
Bam!

The shoe stamped
down on the stone. Ow!
The stone was sharp and
cut the shoe. The shoe
limped away.

Fred scuttled to his love. "Will you marry
me?" he asked.
"Of course, my darling," said the
beautiful lady woodlouse.
They got married right away and lived
happily ever after. The end.

"It's true," sighed Fred. "It was love at first sight."

Fred and Mrs Fred rubbed antennae.

"What a lovely story," said Ellie. "It is very romantic."

Stamp, stamp!

"That's not right!" cried an angry voice. **"That story's rubbish!"**

Ellie looked around and frowned. "Who said that?" she asked.

"I did!" said an old blue shoe lying on the path. It looked grumpy, as if its laces were in a knot. **"I'm not a bully or a monster. Why should I be the baddie in the story? It's not fair.**

No one cares about my feelings."

"You should see things from my point of view," said the shoe. "How would you like to be cut by a sharp stone?"

"Well, I wouldn't," said Ellie. "But I wouldn't like to be squashed flat either."

"That's right," agreed Fred and Mrs Fred.

"It's not my fault. It's the person who wears me who's to blame," argued the shoe.

"Anyway, who cares about creepy crawlies? They're all pests." He stuck out his tongue at Fred and Mrs Fred.

"What rot!" cried Mrs Fred. "We are not pests! We are good for the garden."

"Yes," Fred added. "We eat dead plants and vegetable peelings. Then they come out the other end in our poo and feed the soil, which helps new plants to grow."

"That's right, dear," Mrs Fred agreed proudly. "People recycle bottles and cans; we recycle nature."

Yum yum!

"I didn't know that," said Ellie. "That is good."

"Hmm." The shoe shuffled impatiently.

"Why don't you tell us your story?" said Ellie.

"About time too," said the shoe.

35

The Shoe's Story

One day, a big, blue, beautiful, shiny new shoe was walking down the garden. He had just been given a new pair of stripy laces and he was feeling very happy. Suddenly, a *silly* woodlouse came out, *without looking*, right in front of him. The shoe tried to pull back, but it was too late.

Down he went.

The woodlouse curled into a ball and rolled away. The shoe landed on a sharp stone.

"Ow!" shrieked the shoe. He was badly hurt. The woodlouse got away without a scratch, but the poor, brave shoe had a big cut and lots of scuffs. He had to go to the cobbler to be mended. But he was never the same again and his fine stripy laces were given to another pair of shoes. The end.

"That is a sad story," said Ellie.

"I think the shoe got just what he deserved," said Fred.

"Quite so, dear," said Mrs Fred. "Big bully." And with that, the two woodlice disappeared.

"Insects!" tutted the shoe.

"They're not insects," Ellie corrected him.
"They're a kind of crustacean – like crabs."

"Oh, really!" huffed the shoe and that was
his last word.

The full moon winked again.

"Supper time, Ellie!" called Ellie's mum.

41

That evening, before bed, Ellie wrote a new story.

"A talking woodlouse!" said her brother.

"A grumpy bully shoe!" said her mum.

"What a crazy story!" they cried.

"But it's true!" said Ellie.

The end.

That's not right!

The moon

Put on Ellie's storyteller shoes.

Listen to how each of the characters in Ellie's tale tells the story. How is each one's version different? Look at how the characters are pictured. Did you notice how they don't always look the same – why?

Fred

Mrs Fred

Can you tell the story from the moon's point of view? What kind of character do you think the moon might be? Helpful, wise, boastful?

Be a storyteller like me!

The shoe

Ellie

Tell a friend about what you did at playtime today. Now pretend you are an ant or the slide in the playground and tell the same story. How would it sound?

Make a woodlouse home and observe.

Find us in damp, dark places.

Find your woodlouse under a stone or log outside.

Place about 2 cm of damp soil in an empty carton. Put a lump of wood on top of the soil. Add some twigs and dead leaves. Next, put your woodlouse inside.

Make small holes in the lid of the carton.

Spray the soil with water and cover.

Check your woodlouse home every day. Spray it with water, but don't make it too wet! After a few days, return your woodlouse to nature.

Woodlouse poo makes good plant food.

Does your woodlouse like light or shade? What does it eat? Watch it walk!

45

Alan Durant

Where did you get the idea for this story? One evening my daughter asked me for a story. I was tired so I told her a very short story about a hedgehog that got squashed by a car. "That's not right!" she said, and she told the story back to me with a different twist. A squashed hedgehog didn't seem very nice, so I changed the main character to a woodlouse instead.

Which character in this story are you most like and why? I am like the moon because the way it looks down over everything, watching it happen, is a bit like being an author. Mind you, some people would probably say I'm more like the grumpy shoe!

What do you do if you get stuck on your writing? I jump up and down and stamp my feet (so maybe I am like the shoe). Then I write something else until I'm not stuck any more.

What did you like to do when you were a child? What did you hate most? I liked anything to do with football plus reading, singing, making up stories and dressing up. I hated eating stewed apple, going to the dentist and getting up early, and I still hate all those things!

Katharine McEwen

Meet the illustrator.

Katharine as a child

How did you paint the pictures in this book?
First, I drew out the pictures. Next, I painted them using watercolours and then drew over the top of them with pencil crayons. It took me about a month from start to finish.

Which character in the story did you most like to draw and why? I liked drawing the woodlouse best, because I enjoyed the challenge of getting it to look like a human character that talks.

Which character do you wish you could be like? I wish I could be like Ellie and make up stories as easily as she does.

What's your favourite place to draw? I like to work in my studio with a nice big cup of tea and a packet of chocolate biscuits!

Did you draw when you were a child? I used to draw all the time, as you can see from the photo of me above, aged two!

Will you try and write or draw a story too?

Let your ideas take flight with

Flying Foxes